JUST LIKE A BUTTERFLY

NEW BEGINNINGS M/M SERIES
BOOK 2.5

KASHEL CHAR

CONTENTS

Title: Just Like a Butterfly - A New Beginnings Novella 2.5

Draft to Digital Electronic ISBN: 978-1-998713-12-7

Draft to Digital Paperback ISBN: 978-1-998713-47-9

Publisher: Koda Calmz Publishing

Editor: Teresa Fornoff

WARNING

No part of this book may be reproduced in any form or by any electronic or mechanical means, including information storage and retrieval systems, without written permission from the author, except for the use of brief quotations in a book review.

This story contains explicit graphic depictions of gay sex and crude language unsuitable for young or sensitive readers or anyone offended by gay sex.

DEAR READER/LISTENER

JUANDRE AND ANDREW APPEAR AS SECONDARY CHARACTERS in the "New Beginnings M/M series."

As Kashel wrote the follow-up to "Here's the Deal," the characters transformed into vampires drinking whiskey.

Since "Here's the Deal" was a true recounting of Stefan Pride's younger days, Kashel shifted the paranormal characters into the New Beginning storyline.

We blamed Ish, who time-traveled.

That is a brief explanation of Kashel's bipolar creative process.

We hope you enjoy the entertaining erotic story of how Juandre and Andrew met.

Love to all creatures,

Kashel Char.

CHAPTER I
JUANDRE

2004 A.D.

United States of America

Interstate seventy-five New York to Lexington, Kentucky

It was a Friday afternoon when I was racing like the Red Queen down the interstate from New York to Lexington, Kentucky, feeling like I would never reach my destination and, simultaneously, reluctant to start my life as a straight-married man and a father-to-be. I was a busted, young, and closeted gay man with a double major in medicine and environmental science. As a Hispanic with stuck-up as fuck parents who only worried about their status and money, my upbringing was as privileged and sad as a locked-up mouse in Fort Knox. This cheese-cake body was going to waste, and I was not getting younger.

When I crossed the bridge at the Ohio River, I made a pit stop at a pub after I saw the Lord Andrew Distillery advertisement on a billboard. The picture of the bourbon made me crave alcohol, so I swung my sexy sports car over to the first R&G—rainbow and glitter—establishment for a martini or three. One olive turned into several before I returned to the highway, wired and waving off my newfound besties, whom I would probably never see again. Their enthusiastic motivational pep talks pushed me to a point where I gave two fucks about what awaited me in Lexington. I needed to get my asshole polished without disinheriting myself before I married a woman who I was certain had stolen my sperm and impregnated herself without my knowledge.

At twenty-two, my existence was crusty, and my new friend Angie Joelee from the R&G I'd just visited, convinced me to search for a drag mother and the man of my dreams.

To this day, I don't know why I didn't face up to it years earlier. I mean, I've only ever been attracted to men, but I loved feeling like a woman. Some days I didn't want to be a woman, just a man, but I still wanted to fuck a man so hard I wanted him begging for my magic wand. My girlfriend, Chrissy Montgomery, was conspiring with our parents. My blood ran cold when thinking about the life sentence I was about to enter, all because my Spanish Roman Catholic upbringing deemed it so, to keep me from ending up in the eternal fires of hell. I didn't recall fucking or fantasizing about fucking the woman, ever. Maybe I wished to rip her Sunday best trappings from her body, but that was to wear it.

When alone at home, I draped myself in diamonds and jewelry and walked around in black fishnet stockings and size eleven Gianvito Rossi black suede Camnero heels. I loved feeling beautiful while I studied; it made it fun, and I seemed to retain more information as I studied when I felt confident. And that was also why I kept it a secret, because when it wasn't a secret, I feared losing the magic. I knew it was silly, but I really needed my parents' money. But since I was getting my degrees, I figured it was time to spread my wings and try them on someone who didn't know me.

With alcohol fueling my lust for a man, I loudly exclaimed into the night, "Lord, if you get me a good-looking man to have sex with, I will go to mass every Sunday for the next year!" I doubted God would ever answer my drunken prayers. Then I remembered some meditation classes I'd taken that summer about positivity and visualization being the first step in materialization. So I described to the Lord precisely what I wanted.

"Lord, if it pleases you, I would like a big man. Straight would be extra nice as long as he doesn't get violent. I don't want him to be overweight, but a teddy bear would be perfect. Maybe a swimmer with a muscular physique without veins popping out all over. It would be okay for his cock to be big and veiny. Tall is nice, too. Above all, please ensure he has strong, hairy legs. I don't care what color eyes he has, as long as they aren't brown like mine. A pale complexion is preferred, but the color of his skin isn't as important as an above-average cock size. I like stubble and a sexy swagger." I kissed the tips of my left pointer and middle finger and sent it into the universe as I howled my prayer into the night.

Minutes later, my prayers were answered. In the distance, I saw the shape of a man materialize. I took my foot off the gas and, as I drove closer, I noticed his arm was out and thumb up like a hitchhiker.

"Damn, what have we here? Come to Daddy," I said and immediately turned my loud music off and slowed the car down to observe the manifestation. I was almost sobered up, so this man with an athletic build standing at the side of the highway was not an apparition but the actual answer to my prayers. He was wearing a baseball cap, had long blond hair, and was in a tight pair of tattered jeans. Sitting next to him on the road was a small duffle bag. He lowered his arm, and I confirmed that, yes, his thumb was up and he was hitchhiking. Which, of course, was illegal, but I didn't judge as the olives sloshed in martinis inside my stomach. I was driving drunk, after all.

Eager to inspect my God-given horse in the mouth, I straightened my neck and batted my lashes as I pulled my little sports car off the road near him. He grabbed his bag and ran up to my car with a genuine smile of relief. I lowered the passenger side window and switched on the interior lights. I quickly did a summation of him. I guessed that his shoulder-length blond hair was sun-lightened. He looked like a surfer or someone being outdoors a lot. His eyes sparkled with a shade of green in the dashboard light. He had a thick dark beard shadow, unusual for a blond. He was about my height but much more muscled and packing what appeared to be a full basket.

"Thank you, Lord," I whispered. I made sure to cover all my bases by being thankful and showing appreciation while making a mental note to attend mass every Sunday for a year, as I quickly scanned the hunk hanging on the side of my car.

"Where you headed?" I asked him, trying not to let my jittery nerves show.

"South, toward Louisiana, and you?" His voice purred deeper than my car. His accent was a mixture of German or Southern drawl, and I was unfamiliar with its origin.

"I'm cutting off from the interstate. I'm heading to Cincinnati. I can take you as far as that." I lied about my final destination and offered a friendly smile while hanging on the steering wheel. I felt cheeky and adventurous, so I batted my eyelashes, showing him how cranking sexy I was. If that was off-putting to him, then I was wasting my time. I'd try the next hitchhiker that came along. But he smiled wider, and I could see he liked me.

"That would be great! I've been walking for almost two hours. I didn't think anybody was ever going to stop. I guess I'm just lucky a state trooper hasn't come by," he said as he opened the door of my car.

"There's one catch, honey," I said with my best effeminate lilt. He paused, and our gazes met.

"What would that be?" he asked with a skeptical look and an uncomfortable chuckle.

"You let me blow you," I said as campy as possible, and I wasn't chuckling. He took in a deep breath and stepped back from the car. I thought he would slam the door and tell me to fuck off.

"Are you kidding me?" he asked. But when he saw my seriousness, the smile left his face.

"No, my boy, I'm not kidding you. I'll give you a ride and rent us a room in Cincinnati. You look like you could use a shower and some rest. In return, you let me play with you a little. Then we sleep a few hours and say our goodbyes," I said in a matter-of-fact tone. Okay, he didn't know what I was planning, and Angie Joelee had just told me to be myself and ask for what I needed and wanted from a man. My preferences were unconventional, and this man looked much older than me, but I was sticking to my plan, and that was that. He stood there with his mouth open, probably not knowing what to say. He'd thought I was kidding but must have realized that no one in their right mind would stop and ask him that. I knew God had really sent him to me when his look of absolute horror melted into a sly, all-knowing expression. He cocked his head to one side like he was checking me out. Then he looked me in the eye, and I swear I could only hear my heartbeat thumping as the world suddenly froze, and all the air and sound got sucked out of our bubble. As inexperienced as I was, I knew this guy, who was probably twelve to fifteen years older than me, was perhaps straight as an arrow, but he wanted this.

"Whatever," he said nonchalantly in his sexy accent. "I'm tired of walking and standing by the highway, praying the Lord sends someone to pick me up."

I told him to put his bag in the trunk as he opened the car door. I remember thinking fleetingly about stories I'd heard of hitchhikers carrying axes, knives, and stuff to kill unsuspecting travelers. With his bag safely in my trunk, he slid into the soft leather passenger seat, slamming the door while never taking his eyes off me. He smelled of sweat, and I found I liked that.

"I'm Sam." I lied about my name and shook his hand casually after asking to blow him.

"Ryan," he responded. The car suddenly felt much smaller as he searched for the seatbelt, clipped it in, and made himself comfortable. Finally, he gestured to go and stuck his arm out the window, riding the wind with his hand. It would be about an hour and a half before we reached Cincinnati, and I didn't think I'd ever been so nervous. I was stunned by my boldness, and it felt great. I couldn't believe that I'd propositioned a stranger. I had a fleeting thought that I may drive, but maybe he was the one taking me for a ride. I kept glancing over at him. He was an extremely good-looking man. Kind of rough around the edges and not the type of person I would usually associate with, but very much all man.

I was at a loss for what to talk about and ended up asking him if he lived in Louisiana. He told me he did and was heading back from Michigan, where he'd been doing factory work but was recently laid off. His odd-sounding accent wasn't German but Cajun. He told me that he had a wife and a teenage boy waiting for him in Louisiana. I thought about how lucky she was to have this hunk returning home and how good it must feel to have him on top of her. I felt my cock, which had been chubbing since he'd first gotten in my car, begin leaking.

His hair was shoulder-length and very blond. Streaks of different shades of gold to platinum fell forward, hiding his rosy prominent cheekbones—

his shyness—from me. We talked about mundane things for a while. The more we spoke, the more I was attracted to him. He was a big teddy bear of a man, and as he laughed, his eyes crinkled at the corners, like someone who laughed often. I asked him what he would do for work once he got home. He said he didn't know and returned the question, asking me what I would do when I got my second degree. He talked about his wife and boy, and I talked about my girlfriend and how we would probably get married one of these days. My mouth had gotten parched. I was nervous, but my confidence grew just as Angie Joelee had promised it would, and so the day turned out to be one of my best days ever. As we sat in the silence, I thought about my proposition and his acceptance. He must have been doing the same, as he seemed to be getting anxious.

Because I wanted to play with him, it was up to me to tackle the awkward quietness in the car. "Please, take your cock out and let me see it," I asked and flapped my right wrist at him as if it was nothing. How would I tell this man I craved submission from older, bigger men? His jeans had a definite lump, and I was even more curious. One thing that I was good at was reading people. It was a natural talent. Little did I know at the time that he was reading me much better.

"Not now. I'm filthy. I've been on the road for days. I'm also not queer. So why do you want to do this anyway?" He coughed and shifted uncomfortably in his seat. I had to take control if I wanted it. He should know what I needed from him, so I needed to be honest.

"I don't know. It's just something I have to do, and you agreed I could play with you," I answered but thought if I didn't spit it out now, it would make things much more difficult, and he might not like it if I was a conniving little shit. He smiled at me as if reading my confused blabbering mind. I straightened my spine. "I don't care if it's dirty or not. I want to see you play with it. I won't do more than touch it, and I can't suck it while driving, can I?"

He gave me a thoughtful look. I was starting to like that about him. His green eyes sparkled with mischief. "Fuck it. Whatever," he said as he scooted down in the seat and unzipped his jeans. He pulled his semi-hard dick through the opening. His penis wasn't huge, but it was a respectable size. As cocks go, it was a handsome uncut one.

I'd never seen one with a cut foreskin, except in magazines or porn flicks. I was fond of fleshy hoods and how they slid back to reveal beautiful satiny heads. Ryan's one-of-a-kind head was perfect. Wild pubic hairs sprung out of his zipper along with his cock. The pubic hair was a darker blond than the hair on his head, matching his beard more closely. I was all lustful and anxious. My teeth chattered. I wanted to get to Cincinnati as fast as fucking right now.

"What do you want me to do?" he asked softly, ripping me out of my stupor. His voice was low; yet for some reason, I thought we naturally fit at that moment. He liked asking me what I wanted. Halleloo!

"You have a beautiful cock. Play with it a little. Move the skin back and forth," I said, trying not to sound overeager and surprising myself with my sturdy boldness. I kept glancing from the road to his cock. Then I noticed he looked at me as if inviting me to touch him. I checked the road and reached over and began fondling him with my right hand. I kept my left hand firmly on the steering wheel. It was weirdly the most erotic thing I'd ever experienced. The moment was intense. No radio, no talking. Just the low hum of the engine and this intimate act between two consenting men. It was the first time I had ever had another man's dick in my hand. I continued to caress it, and it responded, growing both in girth and length. It stayed silky and soft to the touch, but the underlying hardness was very evident. Its growth was impressive, and he probably possessed a very thick, eight-and-a-half inches. At that second, I knew I would be touching other men's cocks as often as possible.

A car honked as it sped by us. I grabbed the wheel to take control of the car, realizing we were crossing the median. "Okay, you can put it away," I said and laughed. He said nothing. I brought my fingers to my nose and sniffed audibly, joking about it. He could use a shower, but I liked the pungent odor. He looked at me with what may have been disbelief or wonder. I knew I had this beautiful older man and was turned on beyond belief. I was looking forward to having both my hands and mouth on him.

When we eventually made it to Cincinnati. I spotted an acceptable-looking hotel and pulled in to ask if rooms were available. They also had some mini-suites with water beds, which I chose. I'd left Ryan sitting in my car while I checked us in. Even though the bored-looking man behind the counter didn't ask me, I made a point of telling him I was traveling with my brother. Why, I didn't know, because if the man had given a shit, he would probably have wondered why I was getting a room with a waterbed instead of two doubles with my brother. As a closeted effeminate gay man, in situations like this, lying was second nature to me.

I returned to my little car, wondering if Ryan would still be there. It would have been a good time for him to pop open the trunk, grab his bag, and be on the highway thumbing for a, hopefully, less demanding ride. But when I got to the car, there he was with his head leaned against the window and sound asleep. I got back in my car behind the wheel and turned the key. The engine revved back to life with its strong, smooth Italian-made purr. Of course, this woke Ryan up. I told him we had a room and that I would pull closer to the entrance. He seemed a little groggy but acknowledged what I said with a nod of his head. After finding a parking spot, we each grabbed our bags out of my trunk and headed in the side door and down a long corridor to the elevators. On the eighth floor, I located our room and let him inside. It was roomy and comprised a business workspace and a large flat-screen TV in both the large bedroom and the sitting room. One entire wall was glass, with a stunning view of downtown Cincinnati and the highway with all its traffic.

But a panoramic view was not what was on my mind.

It was like I suddenly bloomed out of my old skin, and the desires and needs I knew little about were coming to me from somewhere deep inside. I felt like a beautiful butterfly rolling my wings to dry and take flight. Suddenly, I wished I had my fishnet stockings and high heels on. I wondered what he would say. Instead, I rolled my little internal wings back up and tucked them away for another day.

I looked over at Ryan and could tell this room impressed him. It was somewhat mediocre, nothing to write home about. I assumed that my southern man had never stayed in a room like this before. I followed his gaze, which was trained on a massive king-size bed against one of the walls. A sudden loud growling came from his stomach and interrupted my thoughts. No telling when he'd last eaten. Again came a growl. Ryan placed his hand over his stomach and gave an embarrassed little smile. He turned away to have a look at the gorgeous view.

"Sorry, it's been a while," he said in a low, deep southern drawl.

"No worries, it's natural," I said and batted a wrist at him. I walked over to the bathroom and flicked on the lights. The bath was surprisingly large and done in black and white marble. Not only was there a spa tub but a separate shower that would easily accommodate two. The counter was well stocked with toiletries, including toothbrushes, shampoos, lotions, etc. I picked up a toothbrush and paste and walked back into the bedroom. Ryan stood before the window, looking at the traffic moving south to some unknown destination.

"Hey, Ryan," I called to him, bringing him back from wherever his thoughts had taken him. I handed him the toothpaste and brush. "Why don't you go take your shower and shave while I order us up some dinner?"

"You don't need to do that. I can't afford what they must charge here, and I don't want to be more obligated to you than I've already gone and done. So I got me a little money, and I can get something from those vending machines I noticed near the elevators," he protested.

"Don't worry about it, Ryan. You've already agreed on what I want. The fact is, I'm hungry, too, and I don't want to eat alone," I told him as I picked up the hotel room service menu. "Now, go shower. I saw some robes in there. Put one on, but nothing else. I'll get us some food brought up."

"Ah fuck! You're going to go through with sucking my cock, aren't you?" he asked, undignified like he didn't want to hear the answer to his question. His words and body language didn't match. I got the distinct feeling he was putting on a show for me. I loved a good show, so I guess our game had started.

"A deal is a deal, Ryan. Look at it this way. By this time tomorrow, you'll be well on your way to Louisiana. Chances are you'll never see me again, and unless you tell someone, who's to know? Yes, Ryan, I'm going to blow you," I told him with a stern voice I didn't know I possessed. And then some, I thought to myself cunningly.

When Ryan had the shower water going, I was on the phone with room service. I quickly ordered two New York strips, very rare, thought better of it, and changed it to well done, with sides of baked potatoes, sauteed green beans, and Caesar salads. Additionally, I ordered a bottle of red wine, but then I remembered my dinner partner and changed that to six beers in a bucket of ice. Then, as an afterthought, I ordered a fifth of Lord Andrew Whiskey. A plan I didn't even understand was taking over. Explaining this charge to my dad would take some doing, but I would deal with that when the time came. I wanted my man relaxed and happy. Okay, I needed some relaxing, too, to be honest.

Ryan's shower was a long one. I didn't know if he was filthy or just trying to prolong coming out into the room and what lay ahead. I imagine it was more the latter than the former. But in about thirty minutes, the bath door opened, and out he came in a white terry robe with the hotel's logo embroidered on it.

"Feel better?" I asked him.

"Oh, hell yeah! I haven't felt this clean for days. I love showers. I try to take them every day, because when I was growing up, we only had an old tub, and I usually had to share that with my little brother. Talking about water, I love swimming. Do you think I could go for a swim in the morning?" he asked, smiling. At least he smiled until he realized I'd locked my eyes on his shapely lower legs covered in blond hair.

Thank you, Jesus, and I promise mass every Sunday for a year!

Ryan seemed to remember where he was and why. He quit talking about how great it was to be clean, cleared his throat, and tightened the belt around his robe. Then, probably not knowing what to do next, he just stood there.

"I'm sure we can go for a swim tomorrow, but for now, come over here, Ryan." I motioned him to where I was sitting in one of the room's two armchairs. Looking somewhat uncertain, he walked toward me and stood about two feet in front of me. His eyes glinted with mischief. I struggled to read him. Did he want this or not, or maybe he was amused or daring me? "Let me see what I bargained for."

"You are such a good-looking young man. You can have anyone you want. Why do it like this?" he asked, looking down at me with anticipation and yearning in his eyes. He was such a contradiction.

"Ryan, that's what we'll find out. I'm tired of pretending. I'm tired of wearing a mask and keeping everyone but myself happy. If we do this and we enjoy it, then you pay your debt happily. Also, you're helping me to figure out what I like and how to come out of my closet. If you don't want me to do this, you better say so now because this boat wants to float," I said as I slid from the chair to my knees before him. His breath hitched. I looked up at him, waiting for an answer. In this position, his belt line was directly at my eye level. He nodded an unspoken yes, and I slowly moved my hands around his waist and wiggled my fingers underneath the tightly pulled belt.

"I need you to know that I fantasize about many things, but my biggest fantasy is to tell a man what I need from him, and he does it without question. Do you think you can entertain my fantasies tonight? Can you stand there and let me do what I must do?" I asked with a seductively authoritative voice.

He swallowed and looked down at me with a smoldering gaze. Tiny cold water droplets slipped from the tips of his wet hair and sprinkled my face. With his thumbs, he brushed them gently away. The moment was intense, and for the first time ever in my life, I knew what it felt like to be truthful, honest, and emotionally bare in front of another man. My confidence grew. Staying on my knees while he towered over me, I undid the belt and let the ties fall aside. Like a Broadway curtain, the robe opened before me, exposing the first manhood I had ever been this close to all my life.

I'm still grateful that my first intimate contact was with this man. His pubic thatch was wild and massive. This man had no concept of male hair trimming. The dark blond hair grew, probably an inch up the shaft, with most of it fanning out to the crease of his pelvic region. His cock was flaccid, but even so, it was a good four inches with a well-formed pink head at its end. The ballsack was naturally hairless and hung down several inches, with two large balls weighing it down. I took my time just staring at it.

My two hands had gone to the man's ankles of their own volition. I slowly ran my fingers and palms up his muscular, hairy calves. It was like every one of those golden blond hairs was sending electric volts into me. I worshiped his body as I moved my hands, rubbing his legs slowly and gently in small circles. I slowed and applied a bit more pressure so that I might feel the ropes of muscle in his thighs. Near the top of his legs, my hands inched around and grasped the tiny pert buttocks that bubbled out. I gently squeezed as I leaned forward, opened my mouth, and took his semi-solid manhood in.

He hissed softly, and I moaned in approval. I paused my sucking because I had to say something. I jubilated, "Oh, my god, you taste so fucking delicious," and then sucked the cock head back into my mouth. Finally, after all the fantasizing, I had the first cock ever passing my lips. Instinctively, I knew what to do. My tongue lifted the head and played, paying particular attention to the sensitive little "V" at the underside of the cap. Ryan stifled a gasp. His cock was expanding in my mouth. It grew as I teased it with my tongue and slight sucking motions. Now it was hard and long, and he was involuntarily moving it back and forth, his breathing hard and ragged. My jaw stretched to the maximum, and saliva dripped from my mouth. It seemed very large, and, in my inexperience, I gagged.

Embarrassed, I let his dick pop from my mouth, and I stood up, trying to win back my dignity. "Our food will be here any time. There's a blow dryer in the bathroom. Why don't you dry your hair?" I asked. He looked like he couldn't believe I'd just stopped, but he turned around and returned to the bathroom.

"I'm only doing this because I owe you," he said with an all-knowing grin over his shoulder.

I felt like kicking the table for letting my embarrassment stop our play, but I lifted my chin and said, "I like how you were listening to me and not questioning what I said," even though I still needed to explain the whole bloody toy box of Daddy/boy dynamics to him and then ask him to be the boy. But I smiled and appreciated the cheeky swagger in his step. Things were progressing comfortably. It was like it was meant to be. Like finally, the gods were smiling at me. I wished we had more time. I would have liked to test my fishnet stockings and heels on him. But I decided to be happy with what I'd already achieved.

Soon, I could hear the dryer. Not long after came a knock on the door, and I opened it to find a handsome young man about my age standing before a cart laden with stainless steel lid-covered plates, as well as the beverages I'd ordered. I showed him where to bring the cart, and he set our table with a linen cloth and even a candle. I had a very obvious erection tenting my jeans and a wet spot showing. He noted it and smiled knowingly at me, man to man.

At about that time, Ryan walked out of the bathroom and into the sitting area, still wearing his robe. His ash blond hair, now dry, hung in waves cascading to his broad shoulders. Although his robe was closed, it, like my jeans, was tented. My poor server's mouth dropped open, and his face reddened. Hurriedly, he finished setting our little table and handed me the ticket. I signed it, giving him a very generous tip and a wink. He thanked me and left.

"Let's eat. I'm hungry, too," I said to Ryan as I walked over to the dining chair and pulled it out for him to be seated first. He looked at me with both surprise and discomfort in his eyes. After I'd helped him with his seat, I walked to the other side of the table and got situated in my chair directly across from him. I could see the hunger in Ryan's eyes as they swept over the table before him. His gaze lingered on the thick succulent steak and the steaming baked potato. I could see an appreciative grin spreading on his face when he spotted the silver ice bucket full of bottles of German beer. Then, again, I heard the rumble from his gut; he enthusiastically reached for his fork and knife and began to cut into his steak.

"Thank you, this looks mouthwatering," he said.

"You're most welcome." I shifted and moved to the front of my seat. Suddenly nervous as fuck. "I thought while we ate, we could discuss our arrangement so both of us know what we can expect and what's allowed. I admit I'm one hundred percent inexperienced, and you appeared exactly when I decided to wash myself of this dreadful virginity. I'm twenty-two and about to marry a woman I thought was my friend, but somehow she managed to get pregnant."

He burst out laughing. "Come on, we all know how babies are made. The boy puts his little worm in the girl's apple and wiggles it around. Apple rotten, babies appear," he said, shoving half a cow into his mouth. I straightened my back, ready to defend my honor. He laughed. It seems my posturing amused him.

"My worm never went into or near any apples, holes, or vaginas. Our parents are Roman Catholic, and being gay, having a baby out of wedlock, or having a simple abortion are all reasons to be burned at all nine levels of hell. Plus, I need to finish my studies. I may be a spoiled brat, but I'm not a liar or a slut." The more animated and loud I got, the more he laughed. Until I realized he was joking with me. "Let's look at this as a night of exploration and expression of our true selves. You said you have a wife and a kid. Tell me, are you into this? I don't want to go into this thinking I can share some of my deepest desires with a stranger and end up being chopped up, butchered, or strangled because he had a sudden attack of manly straightness. I want to know how far you will allow me to go," I said honestly.

He seemed to think it over as he chewed and swallowed. I watched his Adam's apple bob up and down. "Okay, kid, just what am I supposed to do?" Ryan asked.

Damn, he looked so hot in that terrycloth robe that was open enough at the top to show a nice covering of dark blond hair on his chest. I hadn't started to grow chest hair yet, and I was glad for it. Realizing this as an opportune moment, I laid my cards out for him.

"First, don't call me kid. For the next twelve hours or so that we're together, I want to be your Daddy, and you will be my boy," I said and held his stare so he could see I wasn't joking. Strangely, I didn't notice shock or surprise. His green eyes pinned mine, and his pupils covered the green in his eyes. He liked it. So I continued while I was on a roll. "You may call me sir or Daddy. For tonight." For a second, I forgot the fake name I'd given him. "Tomorrow, or when we're not playing, you may call me Sam, not kid," I said and felt guilty not telling him my real name, which was Juandre Martinez, and one of these days, it will be Doctor Martinez. Yes, this was safer. I changed the subject so he could think about an answer. "I hope you like this meal. This combination is one of my favorites."

He gave me a quick nod. Then, we began eating and making conversation like we were old friends.

"So, Ryan, why didn't you take your wife and son up north with you when you got a job?" I asked and cut into my steak. It was juicy inside the charred seasoned crust.

"If the job had lasted, I would have..." I frowned at him. He added, "Sir," and I nodded approval. "I was making pretty good money. I just stayed in a little guesthouse near the factory. I walked to work, so I didn't need a car and sent all but a little food money back home, sir," he said and waited for a cue from me. I smiled and gave an approving nod.

"How long were you doing that?" I asked, somewhat touched by his sacrifice for his family. I was growing fonder and hotter for this working man than I had ever been for any fantasy.

"Just about six months. I started getting good benefits and worked all the overtime I could. Then one day, I showed up and was told they had laid me off. I should have known it was too good to be true. It's the story of my fucking life, sir." All the while, he had already sucked down one beer, and I offered him to have another, which he took without hesitation.

"Thank you, this is the best meal I have ever had, and that beer sure is good," he said, looking down and then added, "I used to drink German beer— sorry, that's not why I'm here. I'm here so you can use me. You don't want to hear about me. It's all about you tonight," he said, and I didn't know if that was sarcasm. So I just ignored what he said. After all, it was all about me.

"Why boy?" he asked innocently. "It's just that I've never messed with a boy before. I reckon I've never even thought about it before—how I was raised. Don't get me wrong, I'm not claiming to be a religious man, but my father was, and he said your kind is an abomination. You being almost young enough to be my son makes it worse, sir." Ryan looked down. His inability to hold my gaze told me between the lines that his father had pulled the religious card on him, as well.

I recognized the same suppressed urges in him. Call it queer intuition. Call it gaydar. I just knew. Unfortunately for our fathers, I wasn't intimidated by that. I figured a little more beer and then some whiskey after dinner would make him agree with me. At the same time, I didn't want any alcohol-fed self-righteousness to make him go psychotic on me or, even worse, give him a limp dick. That would be as counterproductive as a fish needing a bloody bicycle.

It was time to bring on a reasoning strategy. So I decided to throw the Joker card at him, as it was time to do more convincing. "Look, Ryan, try to look at it from my way of thinking. I'm not lying when I tell you I have never done this or anything close to it with a guy or girl. The only sex I've ever had was with my hand, which I enjoy. But I have these feelings, thoughts, and fleeting visuals that I'm on stage and wearing drag." His eyes enlarged, but I stumbled on—no need to stop now. "I've got to find out if I'm queer or not and to what degree. If I like it that much, then I'm willing to disinherit myself and work for fucking Doctors Without Borders. Not that I think drag queens are welcome in Uganda. Okay, let's skip Uganda. My point is, I'm fucked in the head and desperate. I need you to help me decide how I will raise my child. You're literally going to help me decide what to do with the rest of my life. I chose you because I have a gut instinct that you're a good man. Because if I'm so gay...so fucking queer that I won't ever be able to touch my future wife, I want to be able to go home tomorrow and tell her with full confidence of that. Plus, there aren't any laws here anymore that make queer sex illegal." I hoped I was making headway.

He nodded and seemed to agree, so I lowered my voice, looked him up and down, flung my hair to the side with a flick of my neck, and narrowed my eyes to smoking-hot levels.

"Also, being older means you're not going to tell

everybody about this like some straight punk my age is liable to do. So don't you see? You will be helping me a lot, and in return, you're helping your family by doing this so you can get home faster to them. My reward is two-fold. I get to find out about myself, and I get to help out a nice man like you by giving him a place where he can rest comfortably for a while, have a marvelous meal and a couple of drinks, and probably feel really good from what you're going to let me do to you," I said this with all sincerity as I purred at him seductively.

Ryan swallowed and seemed to grasp what I was saying. He was just a little backward. But I saw intelligence in his eyes. And I knew that if I could shift the responsibility of what was happening and make him understand he was doing it for a good reason, he might convince himself it was okay, and we might have one hell of a good time. Those required psychology courses may be paying off.

Ryan spent a good several seconds thinking. He took another swig of beer, finished it, and grabbed another before he spoke. "You think this could help you? If you find out you like sucking dick, do you really think this will help you?" he asked.

"Ryan, I know it would. Please believe me."

He shifted uncomfortably and opened the beer,

shaking his head. I'll never forget those big, inno-
cent green eyes when he looked up and answered
me. They reminded me of moss-covered rainforests.
With the light flickering, the dark green and yellow
specks seemed to move. Sometimes they even had a
green sheen to them.

"Okay then, I don't mind helping you and maybe
paying you back for the ride and food," he said with
a nod of his head and another swig of beer as if he
was sealing a deal with himself. "But I don't understand this sir and boy stuff. Why can't you just suck
my cock and see if you like doing it?" He pointed his
beer at me in question.

I anticipated that question. This man was pretty
smart. The fact was, this had taken over the conversation and was keeping me with a rock-hard
erection.

"Well, boy, that's a part of it. I watched a bit of
gay porn, and some men are into what's called being
dominant. They're called the Dom for short and are
often into a little bondage and discipline. You know,
cuffs, ropes, or ties. It turns me on when I see men
doing that and being completely satisfied. Both
men, the one submitting and the one dominating. I
believe I'm one of those men, but it depends on
what I find out tonight and why I hoped you'd let

me explore that with you," I explained animatedly—
I believe it's called campy.

"I don't know. I mean, I don't even understand
everything you're telling me. But I gave you my word
to help you, and that's what I'll do," he said with
sincere determination.

I cocked my head and looked at him.

"I mean, that's what I will do, sir!"

I smiled when I knew he was back in my game. I
almost exploded in my pants whenever he did that
sir thing. I had a feeling he knew it.

"So, boy, tell me about growing up in the south?"
I asked him.

"Not much to say." I gave him a look. "Sir," he
quickly added. In between hearty bites of food, he
shared more of his life with me. "There was six of us
kids—a pretty small family for that part of the country. My ma was just a kid of fourteen when she had
me. After that, she had one 'bout every year. About
half of them died when they were born or a little
after. Ma died when she was twenty-five, just worn
out, I think. Pa was a hard worker but could barely
read 'n write. He just got to the fourth grade, I guess.
He was really hard on me. He had what my old
granny called a natural mean streak. He claimed he
wanted to make a man of me. He never put much

faith in books. I made it to the tenth grade because the county made him send me to school. Didn't stop him none from making me work mornings before I went to school or until dark when I got out of school on our farm. It was more swamp than farm. Not many nights went by he didn't beat me for something I'd forgotten to do or maybe the way I answered him or looked at him. So when I turned sixteen, I left for Louisiana. Later I heard that the county had come in and taken my brothers and sisters away. I don't know where they are, but I think they're better off than where they were. So I picked up whatever work I could find and did okay for myself. Then I met Barbie, my wife. We were just kids, barely seventeen years old, but we got married and had my boy right away. That's all I'm going to have, though. I can't afford him, but I'll do whatever I have to do to make his life better than mine. My son is sixteen, not much younger than you, and he's talking college. I can't even imagine a kid of mine going to college. But I'm going to do everything I can to help him do that, even if me and my wife have to sell our blood to help pay for it. That's pretty much my life. Not very interesting, is it, sir?" He finished this recount with a bittersweet smile on his handsome face.

"What do you think he'll do with college?" I asked him. While I couldn't relate to this man's pain, I could feel pity for what a difficult life he'd endured. The interesting thing was that it hadn't beaten him down yet.

"I don't know. I want him to be a good man who can make a good life for himself and his family. I know he'll never drive down a highway and pick up a man wanting to suck his cock. Not to be disrespectful, sir!"

I had to admire his honesty. With those words, he had unknowingly entered another part of my game arena.

"Well, boy, I hope you're right. Just like you not wanting your kid to go through what you went through, I hate the thought of a kid in an intolerant society going through what I'm going through," I told him evenly. "However, I want you to know I found that very disrespectful. You may have to pay for that." I looked him dead on when I said that.

"Look, kid...sir, let's get on with what you started before dinner. Then we can get some shut-eye, and in the morning, you can get me a little further south," Ryan said. Did I get a tone of wanting to finish what we started before dinner?

"Patience, boy. Let's have a drink of Lord Andrew

to bolster our nerves," I suggested as I got up and poured a shot for myself and a healthy shot for him.

He frowned and jumped up. "What did you just say?"

I handed it to him and tipped my glass up, and swallowed the harsh burning liquid in one gulp. Ryan looked at me strangely, lifted his triple shot, and in two swallows, it was empty.

"I said I'm nervous. I bet you are, too."

He frowned and put his glass down. Little did I know, Ryan also gave me a fake name that night.

The tension in the room built up to suffocating levels. But I continued my game of domination, manipulation, and seduction. "I hope you don't mind if I get more comfortable," I said as I took my keys and phone out of my pocket and set them on the table. I kicked my shoes off and loosened my tie so it hung loosely around my neck.

"I'm going to take my shirt off, too," I said as I unbuttoned it and slid it over my shoulders, revealing a decent gym-made six-pack, smooth chest, and a nice treasure trail leading into my pants. Ryan's eyes were locked on my hands as they drifted down my body to my pants. He looked like a cobra in a trance, and I was happy to charm him.

"Well, what the hell? I might as well shed the

pants. I'll leave the briefs on. I'm sure you've seen your son like that, and I don't want to get my clothes dirty" I unbuckled the pants and slid them off. I couldn't help but notice Ryan's eyes scanning my smooth muscled legs and the prominent bulge in my Klein's. I walked about seven feet from the table and dropped to my knees. I then signaled for Ryan to walk over. As earlier and with a little less reluctance, Ryan stood and walked toward me. His robe was still closed as I put my hands on each side of his hips and positioned him where I wanted him.

I loosened the terry cloth belt and said, "Take the robe off, boy. We have unfinished business."

Ryan opened the robe and let it slide from his shoulders to the floor. His manhood was right in front of my face. His cock was flaccid now, but I had firsthand knowledge of just how big it could get. I've got a pretty good size dick, but I remember hoping that, by some miracle, mine might yet grow to his size. He had one lucky wife getting to have that put in her! I wondered if his boy was as blessed. The dark blond cock hair continued to fascinate me. I liked its unkempt look and the way it spread to his thighs and once again became light blond. The growth became almost luminous platinum as it descended down his legs to his ankles. I placed my hands on those muscled thighs just above his knees and rubbed up the wiry hair. When I reached his hips, my fingers gripped his hard little bubble butt. It was covered in fine hair. My eyes traveled from the base of his cock up the thick blond treasure trail, past his little belly button, where the trail made its way to his pecs, which could have been right out of a magazine. There, the hair fanned out across his chest just as mine would do over the next couple of years. Then I met his eyes as he looked down at me. There was some confusion in those emerald pools, possibly mixed with dread, but I also saw some desire. It was time that my visual worship of his body ended.

"Tell sir what you want, boy," I commanded.

"I want you to suck my cock, sir," he uttered immediately but so low that it was almost a whisper.

"Tell me so I can hear you, boy," I ordered him.

"I want you to please suck my cock, sir!" This time I could hear him. I leaned forward and took just the head of his cock into my mouth, applied a little suction, and twirled my tongue around the cap. He immediately gasped with pleasure. So I released him from my mouth. Already, his beauty had grown in girth and was developing a distinct downward arch on its rise.

"Are you saying you want this kid who's just a little older than your son to suck your cock?" I tormented him.

"Yes, sir."

"Tell me what you want this Daddy to do, boy," I prodded.

"I want you to take it in your mouth all the way to the root, sir."

The dick was no longer a semi-erect arch toward the ground. It was now reversed and had a slight upward curve as it pointed toward his belly, and it was rock-hard. I leaned in again and licked up the underside of it to its cap. Once again, I passed the large head between my lips and laved it with my tongue, and then slid it all the way to the back of my throat. I suppressed a powerful urge to gag. Back and forth, I went on, stopping at the top to occasionally tease the slit from which was leaking pre-cum. I then pulled off.

"Is that the way your boy's momma does it for you, boy?" I asked tauntingly. My victim hesitated. "Answer me, boy," I insisted.

"No, sir. She ain't never sucked me before. She

thinks that kind of thing is sick and against God's will. It ain't never been sucked before, sir."

I couldn't believe my good luck. Not only had I selected an incredibly handsome straight stud but one whose cock had never been in a mouth before. I had a stereotypically masculine man standing naked before me. My plan was in place. Before this night was over, I would destroy Ryan's definition of what made him a man.

But why, I wondered to myself. This poor man, who was already down on his luck and simply trying to reach his family, had done nothing to me. I put those inconvenient thoughts aside.

"But you do want it sucked now?" I asked as I continued to poke at his values. "By a boy, who in your part of the country could be your son?"

"Yes, sir, I do." His voice trembled. Once again, I took his penis, which was enormous and now roped with veins from want, back into my mouth and began an intense sensual blowjob on this back-woods stud. My novice skills were improving by the second. All the books I'd read were genuinely paying off. My nose was diving into the hairs. Though clean, they still smelled of manly musk. The semen oozing freely from his slit tasted sweet, and I used my tongue to spread it about the head over those sensitive nerves.

Ryan was moaning freely and began participating in his pleasure by thrusting back and forth into my mouth. While he wasn't saying anything intelligible, the grunts were saying everything. He'd placed his hands on the back of my head to hold it in place as he continued doing his fucking jabs into my mouth. He was rapidly building to his orgasm. This was going much faster than I'd planned. He, no doubt, fucked his wife like he was fucking my mouth, hurriedly so she wouldn't think he was prolonging the pleasures of the flesh and yet long enough to get his rocks off. While I was psychologically evaluating the situation and getting that succulent dick thrust in and out of my mouth, I felt the rod swelling and the thrusting stop. Ryan's hands tightened on the back of my head, and suddenly my mouth filled with volley after volley of cum.

"Argh," Ryan shouted as he held my head in place, making me take the thick fluid. I managed to swallow most of it, but some escaped around my lips as I tried to catch my breath. I hadn't planned on this. I'd wanted to watch it erupt, but this wasn't so bad. My hands were still grasping his fuzzy ass cheeks. I could feel his body tremble from the orgasm. He pushed in short quick strokes a couple of times until his orgasm had subsided, and with his spent cock still in my mouth, he shouted, "Damn you, boy! What have I done?" He pulled out of my mouth with a plop. "I should never have let this happen! I'm not a man, just like my old man said!" Ryan was like a rattlesnake, upset, angry, and ready to strike. God, almost to the point of tears.

Maybe I hadn't been as lucky as I thought. I just hoped he wasn't the psycho I now visualized. I imagined my parents trying to identify my dismembered body at the City Morgue and that it would be me that was the catalyst for this hitchhiker's killing spree. I suppressed those thoughts and once again went with my gut instincts.

"Chill, Ryan! You did nothing wrong. This is all on me. Remember what we talked about? I talked you into letting me try something. You were helping me." I was desperately trying to get him into a pre-orgasm frame of mind.

"But don't y'all see? I enjoyed what you were doing. I mean, I liked the feel of it. But, at the last of it, spilling my seed, helping you wasn't what I was thinking. My old man was right," he said again, shaking his head.

"So are you saying you want to be with men now?" I asked, knowing the answer.

"Fuck no! I shouldn't have liked you sucking on my dick. I liked it too much, I can't explain why, but there are things I can't tell you. I'm not a real man, sir," he stated, and for one second, I thought I saw longer-than-normal incisor teeth. He turned away, and when he looked back at me, they were gone. I thought it was probably the light or my imagination. I didn't think he even heard himself say sir, but I sure did.

"Okay," I said as I understood completely where he was coming from. "Let me just say I know very few men who wouldn't accept a blow job from another guy no matter how much the guy doing it disgusted them. But just for my own information, what would your old man have done if he'd ever caught you with your dick in a young guy's mouth?"

"He would beat the shit out of me plain and simple, and it would be like God's punishment of me for what I'd done. You won't believe me anyway, so let's leave it," Ryan said, tears spilling from those beautiful eyes and running down his cheek.

"Then that's what we need to do. To make things right for you, I mean." I walked over to the table, poured Ryan another big shot of whiskey, and handed it to him. "Here, drink this down. You're going to need it."

"What are you talking about, sir?" he asked me but slammed the drink down anyway, wiping his mouth afterward.

"You know what I mean! Your old man was right to punish you after you did wrong. Tonight, you just held a barely legal boy's head in your hands and forced him to swallow your spunk."

He was looking at me aghast. "Are you calling the cops, sir?"

"Of course not, Ryan. Why would I? You've got the most beautiful body I've ever seen. I want to use it just for tonight, and you will allow me because you like it, right?" I asked as slowly and clearly as I could.

"I did what you asked me to do. I let you suck my cock, and I played your game. What more do you want?" Ryan asked.

I swear, it felt like he was playing with me.

"Ryan, I know you're not that fucking slow. I just told you what I want. Blowing you and making you come in three minutes was not what I had in mind. I didn't even get to lick your balls, bite your nipples, or kiss you. Please, I want all that and then some more," I asked.

Ryan looked resigned. "Okay then," he said.

"Now get that pretty ass over here and lean over the back of this chair!" I ordered him and pointed to one of the suite's stuffed armchairs. He did as I told him. He lay over the back of the chair with his arms stretched wide and hands braced against the back. His ass, covered in its fleece of blond hair, was sticking out. He was looking back at me to see what was next. He watched me pick my jeans from the floor and pull the belt from its loops. A look of lustful anticipation came on his face as I walked toward him, my prick sticking straight out from me, and I doubled the leather belt in half.

"Your Daddy needs to teach you who's in charge!" I grunted at him and saw him shiver. This turned out to be a night of wet dreams and role-play.

"No, please, please, Daddy, I'll be good for you, don't hit me!" Ryan begged even as I lifted the leather strap and landed it across his ass cheeks.

Thwack! Thwack! Thwack!

Three times I stung his ass with the belt, and he never resisted.

"More! Please, more, Daddy!" he howled over his shoulder at me and winked. What in the ever-loving fuck? This queen was going to town on his ass tonight.

"Tell me what you did, Ryan. Tell me why I have to whip you?" I asked as I lay down another red line over his well-rounded cheeks.

"You must whip me because I forced Daddy to suck my cock and swallow my seed. I promise I won't do it anymore!" That pale, fuzzed-covered ass was bright red now, and a few welts had already formed. Twice more, and then I lay the belt down.

"Do you understand the rules of power exchange, Ryan?" I asked as he continued to stay leaning over the chair.

"I do, sir."

"I just need to clarify that you can't take control. I have to give it to you, and the same for you. You give it to me freely. Also, if you say stop or I say stop, then we stop no matter what." I was clarifying this to make sure he was one hundred percent into this.

"Yes, sir! I understand, sir," he responded sincerely, but he didn't know I could see his face in the mirror's reflection. He was smiling, so I knew he enjoyed our game.

"Well, good then. I'm going to let you finish making it up to me. Hopefully, you'll get some enjoyment out of it, too."

He nodded.

I continued speaking and walking back and forth. When I told him he could stand, I was surprised to see a full erection pointing at me. "I think I may have hit you too hard, Ryan. You have some red welts that will be hard to explain. Go lie face down on the bed, and I'll get some lotion to rub into them," I ordered him. He immediately went to the king-size waterbed and crawled on it, and lay face down. I went to my suitcase and returned with a bottle of lotion, and crawled up on the bed behind him. With my knees, I nudged his legs apart and crawled in between them. The sensation of his wiry blond leg hair against my smooth skin almost made me come. Opening the bottle, I poured a little on my hands and rubbed them together, not enough to absorb the lotion but enough to warm it up. I gently rubbed the lotion onto his muscular globes. Ever so lightly, I rubbed, and I heard him sigh. I was glad it was making him feel better. I did that for a while, and he told me the pain was just a bare throb now, not bad at all.

"When your old man used to beat you, did he make you drop your pants?" I asked softly.

"Yes, sir. In front of my brothers and sisters so they would know what might happen to them," he replied. My cock got even harder with that visual planted in my mind.

"Had he ever rubbed lotion afterward on your ass, like I am?" My question came out ragged because I was getting so turned on.

"Oh no, sir! He'd usually give me a boot in my ass and tell me to get out of his sight. I could hardly wait for that day when I could escape his sight forever," he answered in his low voice, edged with bitterness.

I poured more lotion and massaged his smooth muscular back for a while and then down his hairy legs that I could have rubbed and licked for hours. But I didn't have hours; the evening wore on too quickly. Suddenly another urge took over, and spreading his legs further apart, I separated his ass cheeks and found his little pink hole. If I hadn't known better, I would have placed odds on him going for the latest craze and bleaching. It was so light and, unlike the rest of his ass, hair-free. I knelt down and darted my tongue at it. I heard a quick gasp from Ryan. I darted one more time and then stuck my tongue in him as far as I could. I worked around it and in it. Ryan groaned and was going mad with pleasure. I was thrilled to learn my tongue had that much power. I'd read about this in gay erotic literature that I'd managed to get, but I certainly never thought I would be doing it myself. It just seemed too taboo even for me. Nevertheless, I found myself enjoying it.

"Okay, big boy. Turn over onto your back. You're not going to cheat sir out of playing in front."

He did as told.

"Put your hands behind your head and keep them there." With the man on his back and his fingers laced together behind his head, I nudged his legs apart and situated myself between them. I slowly rubbed my hands up and down his legs. It was hard to explain how the springy hair felt against my palms. It was an exhilarating electric shock feeling that magnified exponentially as I laid my upper body between his thighs. His cock was fully erect, and its natural arch kept it from touching his body except at his belly button, where the tip rested. I could see it throb in sync with his heartbeat. I didn't know how big his dick was, and it's doubtful that he, unlike most men, had ever considered measuring it, but it was pretty impressive. In retrospect and with quite a bit of experience later, I would wager that it was a solid nine inches and quite thick.

"Do you want to beg sir to lick your balls, boy?" I

asked him while my cheek rested against his left thigh, and I'm sure he could feel my moist hot breath on his large nutsack.

"Yes. Please, sir, I'm begging you not to make me wait. I hate the sin you're forcing on me, but I hate waiting for you to do it even more! So please, sir, I beg you to do what you will do anyway." He was begging.

He drank, he swore, and his voice was deep and manly, but someone had ingrained him with so much religious mumbo jumbo that I wasn't sure if he would ever be able to live without guilt for playing my game. Oh well, he'd either get over it or not. I was doing this for me.

I moved my head forward a couple of inches and stuck my nose against the satiny smoothness of his sack, and I inhaled deeply. The odor was of clean soap with a hint of the musky sweat that was already beginning to reclaim that part of his body. To me, it was utterly euphoric. I started licking the two orbs as they lay confined in their protective covering. I saturated them with my saliva. With every lap I made from under his ballsack up to the base of his cock, he rewarded me with a grunt of pleasure.

After a bit, I started licking his cock from the

base to the tip. His slit was leaking profusely and filled his belly button with clear liquid. Recalling how sweet that nectar had tasted earlier, I couldn't help but spoon it out with my tongue and lave it over his cock head. I then took the staff in my hand, held it perpendicular to his body, and lowered my mouth on it. Greedily, I twirled my tongue around the corona of his cock and took back the liquid I'd just painted it with. Slowly, all the while willing my throat muscles not to rebel, I took his cock beyond my tonsils and deep into my throat, which was no minor feat due to the natural curve of his penis. Then applying some suction, I began to ease his colossal manhood from my mouth. While I was doing this, Ryan was grunting and moaning with the pleasure his body gave him against his will.

"Boy, sir's permitting you to talk."

"Yes, sir," he responded, sounding dazed.

"Good. Then the rules are set." I started giving Ryan head again. I used my tongue to play with his piss slit, and then once again, I began practicing my oral technique on his staff. After a few trips up and down his pole, Ryan started moaning before he started to verbalize.

"Oh yeah! That feels so fucking good, baby. Ah! Oh, my fucking god, ah!"

I must admit I was getting turned on by the fact that I was the man eliciting these words from this straight older man, even though he probably was fantasizing about some woman. If I'd had one more day and night with this man, I would have played a different game. A game in which I was a boy trying to please his Daddy, but for now, I wanted the experience of being the Dom of an older man. So I decided to let Ryan continue racking up punishment for a bit longer, he did forget to say sir. I kept sucking his meat, intentionally making loud slurping noises. Then, finally, I took his dick out of my mouth with a large wet sucking pop and immediately began to nuzzle his ballsack up with my nose so I could lick the area between his hole and scrotum.

"Fuck yeah, that feels good. Lick there some more. Can you get your tongue in my asshole again? Ohm! Yeah, that's it. Stick it in there a little." I was doing what he asked, and sinful or not, he knew what made him feel good. So I moved back to licking his nuts again while I used a hand to push his skin back and forth along his thick shaft in a slow jack-off motion.

"Yeah, keep going! That feels so fucking nice!

Okay, you little cocksucker, put it back in your mouth and use your tongue but keep jacking me."

I did as he said, inwardly smiling. I was certainly looking forward to punishing him again. "Oh fuck, I ain't gonna last much longer. You gonna swallow my stuff again! I got a mouthful for you, my pretty little fairy." Then, with a wet pop, I was off and squeezing the base of his cock so he couldn't cum.

"No, you're not," I said. "This time around, you'll come when I want you to and not before." He was still lying on his back, hands behind his head, staring at me like I was a complete mystery.

"What's wrong? I thought I was doing what you told me. Talking to you about what I was feeling." He said that like he wanted an explanation. It was about then that I released the pressure from the base of his manhood, which was still very much erect, albeit somewhat purple.

"I told you I was giving you the freedom to talk, not to take control." I saw the understanding show in this beautiful face and eyes, followed quickly by a look of dread. No doubt he was thinking of possible consequences for whatever the disrespects were.

"I thought the belt whipping would have taught you something," I continued as I got up from the bed and walked toward my piece of luggage.

"Please, you won't use the belt again, will you? My ass is still burning from the whipping you gave me. I'm still not sure what I did wrong. I thought you wanted to know how what you were doing to me felt," he said in almost a little boy's whine. He was definitely in the process of changing from a macho southern country-man to being wholly dominated—and by me.

"I'll tell you what you did wrong," I said as I returned to the bed, having retrieved from my luggage what I wanted. My cock was raging hard. It was starting to hurt from such a prolonged erection.

"First, you forgot that I'm your sir. As I recall, you substituted fairy where you should have said sir. I'm not your fairy. I'm your Dom, which, boy, is short for Dominator. You are mine tonight to please me and not insult me by calling me a cocksucker, like it's something bad, and calling me a fairy. You want me to go on about what all you did wrong?" I didn't wait for an answer.

"To answer you, boy, I thought about using the belt again. But the truth is, I do like you, and I don't want to hurt you to the point you have scars. From what I've read, that's not what a good Dom does. Besides, the belt didn't seem to help you that much. I'm getting about as frustrated as your father must have gotten with you. Maybe you were a bad boy, and regardless of the punishment, you've grown into a bad man," I lectured him as I crawled back on the undulating water bed.

"I'm not a bad man," he pouted. "I think the belt helped, but I'm glad you won't do it again."

"Are you willing to prove that you're not a bad boy and that your Daddy hasn't wasted time trying to teach you?" I asked, all the while rubbing my hand up and down a fuzzy thigh. "Do you want me to stop?" I asked and changed the tone of my voice so he could understand this wasn't part of the game.

"No, Daddy," he said shyly.

I nodded at him, and he nodded an unspoken yes back at me. So I continued. "Do you want to please your Daddy?"

"Yes, sir. I want to please you. It's just, at the same time, I keep thinking, what if my granny and your parents were right, and this will make us all go to hell?" He moved his eyes in different directions.

Fuck he's good at role-playing!

"Boy, I've already told you some of this, but I can teach you to be a good man and how to please me and at the same time be punished for the sins if they are sins. Are you ready to put all your trust in me, boy?" I gave him a little pastoral wink and at the same time, placed a finger on his piss slit and swiped off some semen which I rubbed against his sensitive cock head.

Ryan shuddered. "Yes, sir, I trust you."

I nodded and then proceeded to blow him. A minute later, I took my mouth off his cock and straddled him so that my cock and balls were lying right against his. It must have felt as good to him as it did to me because he moaned and moved his pelvis to cause a little friction while I suppressed a moan myself. I leaned forward and nibbled on his small tits one after the other. The hair on his hard pecs tickled my chin and smooth chest. Almost immediately, his nipples were hard and erect. I glanced up at him and saw his eyes were closed, but he was making little throat noises and would thrust his pelvis in a way that rubbed his dick against mine.

"Are you ready to be punished?" I asked as I moved upright and adjusted myself so that his hot long cock head touched the back of my balls and the shaft was semi-wedged between my cheeks. I noted that I had pre-cum dripping on his belly, its sticky substance matting his treasure trail and making it look darker.

"I think so, sir. Just no belt, please," he added.

"No belt, boy, at least not to whip you," I assured him. I got off of him and told him to lie on his stomach.

"Okay, boy, I need you to put your hands behind your back. Sir is going to tie them together. Not so tight it hurts, but just so they're secure. Even when I have you turn over onto your back, it shouldn't be too uncomfortable because the waterbed will give enough so that they're not bearing all our weight."

He nodded, telling me it was okay. Out of the handful of supplies I'd gathered from my luggage, I grabbed a designer tie, which was the only one I had, and bound his wrists together in my best Boy Scout knot. I tested it. There was no way he could quickly work his way out of that if he suddenly had a change of heart. As masterful as I was acting, I still had visions of Ryan freaking out on me, and though I was no slouch, I didn't want this butch factory worker getting his hands around my throat. I also had a relatively long nylon strap that I often used to bind my luggage for flying. I used it on each of his ankles, with one end being in a noose knot. That could be useful if my plan got that far. Until then, his legs were pretty free. With that part completed, I leaned over, moved the silky blond tresses aside, and kissed the back of Ryan's neck.

I whispered his importance of being a good boy and strong man between the kissing and occasional nibble. The next minute, I told him how much he was helping me end my confusion. I was sending him such mixed messages that he had no idea what to think. I got down to his cute little butt again and told him to lift it as much as possible. I helped him balance on the shifting waterbed so he could tuck his knees under his stomach. I repeated my earlier act of licking and probing his little rosebud. I drove him mad, and I loved it.

"Okay, boy, time to roll over onto your back."

He did with little effort, and now he lay there looking up at me, hands under his back and dick hard as ever. I put his cock back in my mouth. It seemed I couldn't get enough of that sweet pre-cum. I held the massive penis in my hand and rubbed the leaking phallus around my lips like it was lipstick. Then I crawled beside the man and lowered my lips, smeared in his fluid, right onto his lips.

"No! No kissing! I may be letting you do things to me with your mouth, but I ain't kissing a guy," he yelled at me as he turned his head aside. Then, he attempted to get up but failed. I enjoyed seeing him struggle with his hands tied behind him while wobbling on the waterbed.

"Boy, you're mine now! You will do exactly what I want when I want to do it. You agreed. Are you going to be good and let me kiss you? Or should I give up on you and leave you lying here like this for the cleaning lady to find in the morning?"

"No, sir. Don't do that. I'll do what you want to do. I'm sorry, sir. It's just that the way I was brought up, it was better to suck a dick than to kiss another man, sir. It just took me by surprise, sir, that's all."

Oddly, I'd encountered that in other straight men since. They would let me suck their cock, and they would suck mine, but if I tried to kiss them, they drew the line. I even had one tell me that he would suck me off, would let me fuck him, but he wouldn't kiss a man. Go figure.

I'd done the right thing by tying his hands behind his back.

"Okay, boy, I'm not a bad person. I'll be generous and give you another chance." I crawled back up onto the bed. "I think we should kiss and make up. Don't you?" I asked him, smiling.

"Yes, sir," was all he said.

"One other thing that I want you to do beginning now. Don't always say sir; try to say Daddy sometimes because that's what I am to you. Now I want you to quit crying and give me a big smile.

Because Daddy is in the process of making you a good man." I ran my fingers through those silky blond tresses and cradled his head with one arm.

"Yes, Daddy," Ryan responded in that beautiful southern drawl, and he smiled. I lowered my head and once again pressed my lips to his. I probed his lips with my tongue while I was reaching down to stroke his cock. Our little disagreement had made him lose some hardness, but as I stroked it, he became as rigid as before. Finally, his lips parted, and he allowed my tongue entrance. We deep kissed like this for a long time, all the while I played with his staff, my rigid cock lying on his thigh. When our lips finally parted, he was reluctant to let my tongue go. He had such succulent pink lips I couldn't help but press back against them and kiss him one more time. Before I pulled completely away, I let him take my lower lip between his as he licked it.

"Was that so bad, boy?"

"No, sir. It felt delicious, Daddy," he answered softly. I reached over to the nightstand and got the rest of the paraphernalia I'd gathered. In my hand, I had two paper binder clips. "Now, boy, these are going to hurt at first," I said with a sadistic grin. Before he could question me, I clipped one first on his right nipple, then his left nipple. Ryan sucked in his breath from the sudden pain. I pulled at one, and he gasped.

"Please, sir, those hurt. I don't like them!" he protested.

"I know, boy, but then I didn't like being called a fairy and a cocksucker when you were pumping your dick in my mouth. It just seems the world is full of things we don't like," I said as I twisted the other clip, which elicited a yelp.

"I have an idea, boy. How about I suck your meat some more? Think that would make your little nubs feel better?" I asked enthusiastically.

"Maybe, Daddy!" Ryan was becoming a man who loved having that big cock sucked, and I was happy to oblige.

"Good. This time, though, there will be a little twist, just like there was to our original deal." I saw the dread come into his eyes. "Now, don't start worrying. You get all upset way too easily. Remember, just a little while ago, you told me that it was better for a man to suck a man's cock than for two men to kiss. Well, guess what? You've gone a step further and kissed a man, and I might add, did a fantastic job doing so. In your way of thinking, we'll take a step back, and you'll have the opportunity to suck some young cock while I'm taking care of yours. That sounds good to you?" I asked my southern man.

"Yes, sir," he answered after not too long a pause. I decided I would let the pause pass this time as I climbed over him and set my butt over his face.

"But before we start, I thought you might enjoy doing a little tongue play with my ass just like I did yours." I'd placed my asshole right over his beautiful lips. I waited. Finally, I felt his tongue begin to lick and probe the part of my body that even I'd never seen. I couldn't help but moan in pleasure as he entered me. When he heard me, his licking and probing got very ambitious. It was like he wanted to please me as I had him. Now I knew what all the fuss was about. This felt damn good. I just stayed in my position and enjoyed this for several short minutes. I then stretched down Ryan's body, rubbing my smoothness against his heavenly blond chest hair.

I moved my lower body back just enough that my cock was at his mouth and my head forward enough that his manhood was again at my lips. As I opened it to take his enormous column in, I felt the moist warmness as he tentatively took in the head of my penis. Maybe I did have to force a man the first time I got head, but I was in heaven. As his tongue licked around my dickhead, I thought I would blow immediately.

Somehow, I managed to hold on as I felt more and more of my shaft sinking into Ryan's mouth. Suddenly he gagged. I thought he would vomit, but he regained control and held it where it was momentarily. Then he started sucking again, teasing my piss slit like I had his. My southern country boy could not only charm me out of my pants, but he was a quick learner, too. As he got into a comfortable rhythm, so did I. We were sucking in sync. I decided to go a little further, sticking my index finger in my mouth alongside his prick. I got it nice and wet, reached under his scrotum, and gently slid it into his hole. I felt more than heard him moan as the sound vibrated my dick. I moved the finger in and out until I had worked it all the way into his tight ass. I felt a hardness in there, which had to be his prostate, and when I rubbed that, he moaned and wiggled his cute little ass. He kept sucking me as I did him. I worked a second finger in him, and just as I rubbed his p-spot, I reached back and tweaked the paper binder that still gripped his nipple. A loud sound of pleasure and pain came from him. I felt his cock head throb and swell; quickly, I gripped the base and once again aborted his attempt to ejaculate. As much as I wanted another mouth full of his thick cum, I had other plans. I pulled out of his mouth as I released him from mine.

Maneuvering on the waterbed was awkward, but I managed to swing around and straddle his chest; I said, "Okay, boy, open up; Daddy-boy wants to see those sweet man lips wrapped around my cock."

Ryan opened up, and I slid about halfway in and began fucking his mouth. I was leaking by that time, and Ryan was gulping it down. Finally, when I had to grip the base of my cock to keep it from coming, I climbed off Ryan and gave him another kiss. He responded in kind. I ordered him to bring his knees up to his chest so I could lick his ass some more. For a slow-talking southern guy, he moved faster than a New York minute. At this time, I got the strap I'd tied to his ankles, and pulling its length inside between his knees, I looped it over his head and behind his neck. I adjusted the strap so that his knees stayed in place. Then, true to my word, I got down and gave his hole a good tongue lashing, rallied on by his sounds of pleasure.

"Please, sir, don't stop! I ain't never felt anything that good," he told me as I reached the nightstand, brought the condom packet to my teeth, and tore it open.

"What are you doing, sir? Please, no! For a boy, you're fucking big. You'll rip me apart with that."

"Quiet, boy! We're too far into this to quit now. I'll tell you what I've read that's supposed to help. After that, it's up to you if you follow my advice or not. I frankly don't care. My meat is going in that tight ass of yours, like it or not." I laid it out to him like it was going to be. I got some of the lotion, which was all I had, put it on my suited-up dick, and generously applied some to his hole.

"I understand that as I push in, you need to let your breath out and push out like you're trying to shit. I promise I'll go slowly so you get used to me being there. You understand?" I asked him, sounding very sure of myself when I had little idea what I was talking about.

"I'll try, sir." He knew he had little choice. I began to push in. The yelling and pleading started before even half my head was in him.

"Boy, you got to shut up, or someone will call the front desk for security, and believe me, it will go easier on me than you," I warned him. "Once the head of my dick passes your muscle, it won't be so bad, I promise." I believed I was telling him right because the head of my penis was big. I was pretty sure that once that was in, his ass would relax around my shaft.

"Push!"

He did, and I did, and my cock head was in my first piece of ass. I let it lay in him while he got used to it, and his breathing slowed. When Ryan had finally quit grimacing, I eased in another inch and another and another until my trimmed pubes were flat against his ass. I followed this by pulling back about two inches and pushing back in. Each time I withdrew a couple more inches only to push back in, and every time I did, Ryan grunted, in pain or pleasure or a combination of both, who knew? When, finally, I'd pulled out to where just the cap of my cock was in his ass, I let it rest there. I noted that Ryan's staff, which had gone limp when I first began penetration, was starting to get hard again. His eyes were still closed. While I sat there enjoying the hot tightness around me, I stroked his dick with one hand and rubbed his blond furry thigh with the other.

"Ryan, open your eyes and look at me," I ordered. Then staring up at me were those pools of moss green.

"Why, Daddy, what did I do to make you want to

do this to me? You've taken my manhood away from me. Y'all are treating me like I'm a woman." His voice was on the verge of breaking up again.

"Boy, trust me when I tell you you are all man. I would never have been interested in you if you weren't."

"Then why am I liking this, sir?"

He surprised the hell out of me with that question. "I gave you a lot of whiskey, plus you're a nice guy that I convinced to help me out. So don't worry, you'll be back in Louisiana in a couple of days banging the hell out of your wife," I said to him and smiled. "How's that feeling now?" I asked, indicating my cock planted almost balls-deep in his ass.

"Better, Daddy. It doesn't hurt now. It's kind of like you said," he answered. I felt a distinct movement of his hips. In his position, his mobility was limited, but he'd managed to move me about an inch deeper. I gripped each of those muscular thighs for better bracing.

"Hmmm, okay, country-man!" I said at the very instant I thrust my cock hair-deep into him. I began fucking my captive in earnest. Athletically, I was in damn good shape, and I became the proverbial fucking machine. Each time I pulled almost out, only to stop and piston back into his hot ass. With each inward assault, Ryan grunted out a cry. I went a step further. Each time I pulled back, I took my penis out of him and then pushed back into his heat. I was meeting no resistance and thoroughly enjoyed the hot tunnel that encased my cock to its base. Rapidly, I was getting dangerously close to shooting my wad. I pulled out.

"No! No! Don't stop fucking me now. Please, sir. Ram that cock in my ass!" My blue-collar man was begging this preppy schoolboy to use his straight ass.

"Woohoo, country-man! Don't get all excited. I'm not done," I consoled him. "I have a question for you. If I undo your hands and ankles, will you cooperate with me?"

"Yes, sir. I just need you to fuck me." He didn't even hesitate to answer me. This wasn't what I'd planned, but I would adapt and work with it. I unlooped the tie from behind his head, undid the ankles, helped him to his side, and loosened his wrists. I hoped he was a man of his word and wouldn't kill me. Although I was almost to the point where I could die a happy man, I wasn't quite there yet. He rubbed his wrists, red from being tied up, while lying on his back, frowning at me.

"I'm ready, sir. Are you going to finish, sir?" He waited for my direction or approval.

"Okay, boy," I said, nudging his legs apart. It became a reflex action for Ryan. I would touch the inside of his calf with my knee and his legs spread for me. Balancing on the waterbed, I laid my palms on his thighs, then crawled between them.

"Just like last time, but this is your reward for obedience," I said as I raised his knees and asked him to lift his ass. I stuck a pillow under it to thrust at a better angle. My cock knew the way as I slowly penetrated that hot channel. He didn't cry in pain this time, just gasped as I eased all the way inside him.

"I want to lie on you. I want you to wrap your legs over the back of my legs. Use your arms to hold or pull me closer. I want to look in your eyes while I fuck you."

"Yes, sir," he said and grabbed onto my shoulders. I loved that accent of his. I leaned forward, my arms sliding under his sweaty armpits as my ass bucked, driving my cock deeper into him. Our gazes were locked on each other as we sighed together. His rough, calloused hands moved to my ass, kneading my cheeks and pulling me into him. His erect rock-hard cock rubbed between us, making it slippery as his pre-cum mixed with our sweat. I lowered my head and licked at the sweat-drenched hair sprouting from under his arms. Then I brought my mouth to his. Thank god I didn't have to pry his lips open with my tongue. We kissed as if we knew each other for centuries, as our tongues dueled and danced a rhythm of their own.

We shared the taste of his salt in my mouth. The friction and emotional closeness pushed me over the precipice of a deliciously long orgasm. I felt my balls ascend, and then wads of sperm filled the condom. Every time I shot, I tried jabbing deeper into him. Our kiss grew in intensity. Ryan's legs crushed my hips and held me in place. His arms wrapped around my back in a vice grip. My cock, though spent, still throbbed in his ass. I arched my lower back to pull out of him, not wanting to lose the condom inside him. I could still feel his hardness against me. I broke the kiss, raised my head, and looked into his moss-green eyes, then joined our lips again, not breaking the connection. I felt him pushing my shoulders down, knowing he needed me to finish him off without saying the words. I maneuvered back down to where his cock waited, erect and throbbing. I sucked him no more than five times before I felt his manhood expand. For the second time that night, I swallowed his thick cum down my throat. It was beautiful. I moved back up to his lips and shared his sperm with him. I wasn't sure how he would react, but I was surprised when he swallowed and sucked more from my tongue.

After about twenty minutes of just lying there with my head on his chest and his arms holding me against him, I heard steady breathing coming from him. Ryan was sound asleep. I carefully untangled myself, got up, and stood there, naked, looking at him. It was good that we would spend only one night together because I was convinced I was already very much in love with him. If I had a uterus, I would want his babies. I went to grab a warm wet cloth to clean him but decided not to bother him and showered. Afterward, I packed my suitcase, turned down the lights, crawled into bed, snuggled next to Ryan, and slept.

CHAPTER 2
JUANDRE

WHEN I AWOKE AROUND SIX, THE SUN BEGAN FILTERING into the room. Ryan was softly snoring next to me. His face was beautiful in the mixture of light and shadows dancing on his pale skin. It seemed like it sparkled, and his long blond hair glowed. He looked ethereal as he lay exposing half of his naked body, like a 17th-century Bernini white marble statue I once saw as a kid visiting Rome with my parents.

Our night of exploration and discovery was over, and we found most of my answers, but I had yet to reveal my inner self to him. I felt different, much more relaxed, and comfortable than ever with another person in my space. After we cracked our hardened exterior shells—the masks gay men were so accustomed to wearing—we enjoyed the pleasures our minds and bodies craved. I hoped I hadn't added to his problems, at least not for the long term. Maybe his relationship with his wife would be unscathed. I didn't know who his wife was and whether she could fulfill his desires. If he wanted, I would give him my contact details. Even though we would be married, we shared a secret and could be friends, even if it was to support and talk to each other. Or it may develop into something else. After all, he was my first. One thing was for certain—I would have to tell Chrissy who she was marrying.

As quietly as possible, I crawled from the undulating bed and went to the phone in the next room. I called room service and ordered a breakfast of ham steaks, Belgium waffles, hash browns, orange juice, and a carafe of coffee sent up. I also asked them to pack a lunch for the road. After going to the bathroom and pissing, I brushed my teeth and gargled. I estimated I'd slept about five hours, which was a lot for me at twenty-two. I felt good. When I returned to the bedroom, Ryan was awake and lying there with his hands behind his head, staring at the ceiling.

"Good morning, country-man. Did you sleep well?" I asked as cheerfully as I could, not knowing how he would be this morning after I'd used a belt, among other things, on his ass.

"Look, I realize you want to get out of here and on the road as soon as possible. You may not even want to ride with me to Kentucky. If you don't, I understand. I ordered breakfast and asked them to pack you a lunch for later today."

Ryan looked at me. I still had to put clothes on. It completely slipped my mind.

"Well, college boy, y'all changed the terms of our deal, but a deal is a deal, and I reckon you owe me that ride to Kentucky," he said while training those sparkling greens on me. Then he smiled with those Colgate teeth and longer-than-normal incisors and waved me to him. When I got to the side of the bed, he threw the sheet off his naked body and motioned for me to crawl in with him. I did so gladly. He held me in his arms, and I was tingling all over from his touch.

"Sam, did last night help you? Or were you shitting me?"

I almost forgot to respond to him calling me Sam. "Ryan, what you let me do last night was more help than you will ever know. I learned a lot about myself and had fun doing it, I might add," I answered with some visuals playing in my memory.

"So you got to do everything you've been questioning yourself about?"

I lay there next to him, rubbing strands of his hair between my fingers as I thought about the answer to his question. Mostly, plus a few surprises.

"Y'all liked beating my ass with that leather belt? I figure that every time my jeans rub against my rear for a while, I'm gonna remember you. That was as close to my daddy as I ever want to get again," he said with a low growl and smacked my naked glutes.

"Oh, Ryan, I'm sorry about that. I think I carried that one too far. Never in a million years would I have thought I would do something like that," I told him, furrowing my brows in concern. "I enjoyed being bossy more. Dishing out pain is not my thing," I said.

He huffed. "I don't hold no hard feelings about it. I reckon I could've stopped it if I had wanted to. When you said mostly, what did y'all not do?" he asked with interest.

"Well, I didn't wear my sexy nighties and get to shoot down your throat while I held your head in place," I was busy saying when there was a knock at our suite door.

"Oh, man, breakfast is here already!" He sounded disappointed as he held me tighter.

"I'll get the door." I squirmed out of the tight embrace, hopped out of bed, grabbed the robe Ryan had worn last night off the floor, and pointed to his long thick cock lying at an angle across his upper leg. "You just cover that up," I said as I flung my saucy self around to get the door. He chuckled at me, and I confirmed it was room service through the door's peephole, gave him one last look over, and opened it.

"Good morning, sir. Where would you like this?" a different young man than last night asked. He was handsome, probably eighteen, with curly brown hair and a lopsided smile.

"How about over here, and you can take out this dinner cart, please?" I directed him to the dirty dishes from our last meal. He walked over to clear the table of the dirty plate ware and bottles and replace it with our breakfast order. While doing that, he glanced over at the enormous bed, where Ryan was lying on his side and supporting his head with his hand, watching us. The sheet was down to his waist, far enough that a little pubic hair was visible. He greeted Ryan good morning, finished setting our table, and smiled at me.

"Will that be all, sir?"

"Yes, thank you." I signed his ticket, added a generous tip, and walked him to the door. As I shut the door, he looked at me and smiled.

"The night shift guy told me there were two hunks in here. Please don't take this wrong because I need this job, but call Evan if you need a third. Either way, I'll tell the cleaner to come to this room last," he whispered.

"Thank you. I'll keep that in mind." I placed the Do Not Disturb sign on the door and shut it. When I returned to the bed, Ryan stood and stretched in all his naked glory.

"I hope you like what I ordered for us," I told him as I went to the table.

"I think you could order my food about any time, just let me find a clean pair of shorts in my bag and get my jeans on, and I'll be right there," he said. As he walked past me, I saw the welts I'd given him across his muscular ass.

"Do me a favor and eat as you are. That's how I want to remember you. There's little point in getting bashful now. That's not an order or anything, but I would appreciate being able to look at you like that a while longer."

Ryan shrugged his shoulders and came to the

table naked and beautiful. We had an excellent breakfast together—just two naked men sitting at the little table eating and discussing whatever subject came up. Just like any two friends might do, Ryan shared that Canada was as far as he had ever traveled, which led to me telling him about places I'd been. He seemed fascinated and asked a lot of questions.

"I wish I could see Germany again," he said, which I found odd.

"I was born there and had fled to the States." He used his fork and knife to explain it animatedly away. He seemed happy and at ease with me. Something wasn't adding up, but I chose to ignore that. The time we had left together was running out. I didn't want to ruin it for either of us.

"You're still young and would get there if you made a point of it and made it a goal on your bucket list. You come across as an intelligent man, and it seems like if you put your mind to it, I'm sure you could do anything," I said and smiled, ignoring my gut feeling. He was lying to me, but I was also hiding things. We knew each other one bloody day. Exchanging useless superficial pleasantries was supposed to be the norm, but I couldn't help wanting more than that. To learn more about him and stop judging him for not sharing everything with me.

As if reading my mind, he replied, "I'm going to try my best to, I promise. I'll follow up on that with you. Maybe even phone you from Germany and send you a postcard. We can exchange numbers if you want to talk more and get to know each other better," he said and shocked me into silence.

Breakfast was over. I took a final swig of coffee and got up.

"Yes, that would be nice," I said as a fucking afterthought. Great, now he thinks I don't want to see or hear from him again.

"I guess we had better brush our teeth and make sure we forget nothing," I said, walking toward the bath. Ryan followed me in and was taking a piss while I brushed my teeth. When he finished, he walked up behind me. I spat out the gargle and stood up. Then he wrapped his arms around me and laced his fingers on my stomach. I could feel his chest and pubic hair against my back. Placing his head on my right shoulder, our gazes met in the mirror over the sink. We just stood there looking into each other's eyes.

"I was listening when y'all said you mostly got to do everything you'd thought of doing with a man.

You said you still hadn't been able to blow your wad in a man's throat while you held his head in place, and you said something else when the knock on the door stopped you. What were you going to say?" he asked, smiling at me in the mirror.

Fuck, here's the moment of truth. I blushed as I felt the heat creeping up my neck.

"Ryan, it's not important. Besides, the game is over, and I found out what I needed to know, and I'll never be able to thank you enough." I patted his hand, still on my belly.

Ryan nuzzled my ear, first with his nose, followed by his tongue, as he said, "I've got a deal for you if you want to do it."

I shivered. The hot sexy rumble of his breath caressed my sensitive earlobe. "I think I know what you're going to say, and you don't have to do that," I replied as my cock twitched.

"I bet you don't know what I was gonna say, college boy," he replied, wiggling his front against my back.

"Okay, I give up. What's the deal?"

"I'll get on my knees just like y'all did last night and let you pump in my mouth till you blow," he whispered, still looking at me in the mirror. I didn't have to think for very long. It seemed he missed the nighties part of my confession earlier.

"Okay, but what about the sin and hell and all that? Because I'm not the one asking now."

"Well, I thought about that, and if I have to go to hell for all eternity for what I did, I might as well add to the reasons 'cause the sentence sure can't get no worse," he reasoned with a seductive tone.

"Sounds reasonable. Do you want to do it here or in the other room? The other room would be better on your knees, but in here, you can see yourself doing it," I said as my cock sprouted to life. Happy times are here again!

"There's one condition," Ryan said. Where had I heard that before?

"What condition, hmmm?" I asked, enjoying pretending I was walking on thin ice.

"The other thing you said before the knock was that you still hadn't been fucked. I want to fuck you," Ryan said what I was going to say before we got interrupted. Visions of my virgin hole being polished with that enormous cock filled me with dread and want. I expected the pain would be worth it.

"Don't y'all worry. I'll be gentle as possible." Had

he read my mind? I did trust him, certainly more than he could trust me.

"We must be out of here in an hour," I cautioned as I quivered with excitement.

"Time's getting away from us." He smiled. "You want to blow your load first or after?"

Oh, the choices.

"After, I think. I want something to look forward to after the pain," I said.

"You have another rubber?" he asked as he took my hand and led me toward the bed. I always carried condoms but never expected to need them. I got the last two from my bag, handed them to Ryan, climbed up on the bed, and lay down.

"I'd like it if you rubbed some lotion on your asshole and put the rubber on me," he said shyly, but the hunger in his eyes confirmed he wanted me to do this for him. His cock stood at full mast and was already dripping. I ripped the condom package with my teeth. The rubber was extremely tight on him. He needed the extra-large magnum size. While I was confident that Ryan was safe, I hoped the rubber wouldn't break. Although the rubber was slick with lubrication, I placed some on my fingers to smear around my hole. As I slicked my ass, I made a show of it—thank god for water-based lotions.

"No, college boy, let Daddy do that for you. Get on your hands and knees," he said, and I did so. I felt incredibly sexy as I buoyantly, I pushed my perky butt up, laid my head on the mattress, and waited. Switching roles was hot, and I loved it. Ryan squeezed the bottle, dripping the lotion around my entrance, and then slowly inserted what I assumed to be his index finger. His big index finger was rough and calloused. He worked it in all the way. When he hit my prostate, he flicked it, which sent waves of pleasure through me. After working his finger back and forth, he pulled back until the tip remained in me. I heard him spit, and then another joined the first finger. The discomfort wasn't what I had expected, but then, it wasn't what he planned to stick in me. For what seemed like a long time, Ryan worked his two, then three, large fingers around and in and out. Whenever he touched my gland, I sucked in my breath and moaned, thrusting my ass back to get more. He pulled his fingers out. I heard the lotion being squeezed out of the bottle. Then I felt what could only be the huge penis pressing at my hole.

"Oh, my fucking shit, shit, shit!" I cried out and intentionally muffled the sound by screaming into the mattress. Ryan had his hands on each side of my ass, holding me still and balancing himself.

"You okay, college boy? You want your Daddy to stop?" Ryan asked me gently in that strange accent of his. I answered by pushing back hard and steady so his entire cock head passed my muscle ring. Then, thanks to the waterbed, he slid into me another inch deeper.

"Dear Lord almighty!" A flash of white-hot searing pain assailed my body. "Daddy, just hold the fuck still, don't move, please!" I sucked in a breath and tried to concentrate on nothing but relaxing. We stayed in that position for probably two full minutes. Ryan was so patient because I knew he wanted nothing more than to be balls-deep in me. When I no longer felt like he would split me in half, I followed my advice from earlier and pushed out like I was trying to shit.

"Okay, Daddy, push further into me," I said in between heaved breaths as if I was giving birth. He drove in another inch and stopped, waiting for me to get used to the feeling. I had approximately three inches in me and another six to go. This time I pushed back; another three inches slid into me. It wasn't hurting the fuck out of me, and I told Ryan to pull back to where just his head was in me and add more lotion, which he did.

"Okay, Daddy's going back in and trying another

inch," he said, coaxing me. Sweat was beading on his forehead after doing that several times. Then he was in me all the way, and he began lazy, full fucking thrusts. I was doing serious moaning and begging. My cock had gotten hard again after it had retreated during the initial height of the pain. Ryan thrashed into my ass. I learned the distinct sound of his large nut bag banging against my own. He was rushing like I had pictured him with his wife. Trying to finish up before she thought he was having too much fun.

"Slow down, Daddy. Your boy won't have this for a long time, and I want to enjoy my Daddy's cock in your college boy's ass. Let's get me on my back, so I can see you getting pleasure from this boy," I begged him.

Ryan was more than willing. He somehow flipped me over on my back without total withdrawal; that was one advantage of having a long cock. Ryan placed his hands beneath my knees when I was comfortably on my back. He was sitting with his legs folded beneath him. He hoisted my ass by lifting my knees and pulled me toward him until the backs of my smooth thighs rested on top of his hairy ones. We were now positioned so that my knees rested against his upper sides. This move had placed Ryan's cock back to its full depth in my canal. He moved his hands to the base of my thighs near the pelvis and used me to balance himself during his thrusts. He looked from my eyes back down to his cock and watched with pleasurable delight as he moved his meat in and out of me.

"Daddy's boy is making his Daddy feel so fucking good. I've felt nothing that tight and warm and slick on my cock before. If I go to hell for this, it's worth it. How's it feel to you, boy?" He grunted the question as he rutted in and out of me.

"Argh! I can barely stand it. The pleasure is so intense. The pain is still at the entrance, but the curve of Daddy's cock is just right for hitting my pleasure nut. Please don't stop. Fuck this young ass for as long as you want. Please make it last a while longer," I begged. He pushed in as deep as he could and stopped.

"Daddy is gonna stop, but don't fret. I'm keeping you plugged until the tingle in my nuts goes away. Then I'll fuck you hard and fast and then slow and long." My country-man oozed the words out to me in that dialect of his. I looked at the clock and almost panicked.

"Ryan, we're supposed to be checked out of here in ten minutes." It was almost funny watching the disappointment flood over his face. I stretched my arm over to the nightstand and felt for the phone. When I grasped it, I brought it to the bed and dialed the front desk.

"Front desk. How may I assist you?" The desk jockey asked in that very distinct western Kentucky accent.

"I would...Ahh, god!" Ryan shifted, creating more friction against my prostate with his cock. I heard Ryan chuckle while I was trying to decipher what was being said on the phone.

"Sir, what was that?" the confused man asked.

"I...er...am having a few stomach problems. Therefore, I would like to request a late checkout of perhaps an hour or two, maybe three. Would that... ahhhh...be a problem?" I asked raggedly and watched as sweat dripped from his face into the receiver.

"Not at all, sir. I'll notify housekeeping. "
"Th...th...thank you."
"My pleasure."
"No, mine." I hung up, howling at Ryan.

"You did that on purpose, you big dick," I said and laughed.

"Mighta," he said as he started drilling me ferociously. I wrapped my legs around him and pulled his muscled body toward me.

"I know it wasn't part of the deal, Daddy, but you think you could kiss me, or am I just going to get screwed without a kiss?" I asked and laughed, masking my need to feel even closer to him. He brought my laugh to an abrupt end when his tongue entered my mouth. He didn't miss a thrust. It was a mystery how his pelvis could even buck that fast. When he was about to come, he stopped again, looking at me for what felt like an eternity. When he started up again, it was a slow-dancing fuck that included deep, wet kisses, moans and groans, and words of passion.

"Okay, baby boy. Daddy is going to come!" He started power fucking me more than I thought possible. He reached his orgasm, and I felt his cock swell and fill the rubber.

"Fuck me, Daddy, fill my hole!" I screamed while I held onto anything I could grab. His shoulders, the bedding, then one hand on his butt and the other anchoring us on the corner of the mattress. We fucked all the linens off the bed. Under normal circumstances, I would have thought about hygiene and bedbugs, but that was a minor concern. The magical curve of his cock hit my pleasure nut as he pushed in and pulled out. His moans and my grunts were so loud people walking past the door could have heard us, as if I cared! He thrust in as deep as he could, and I felt his whole body spasming as he ejaculated.

"Fuck yes, boy!" Ryan grunted. We were totally out of control. My nuts ascended in my ball sack, and I shot my load between our bodies. We held on to each other, our bodies doing little involuntary jerks as our orgasms subsided. Never have I felt such emptiness as I did that first time when Ryan pulled his cock out of me and felt the limp and warm cum filled condom dragging over my ass cheeks. At last, when he rolled off me, we just lay side by side, covered in both our sweat and my cum.

"What did you think about that, Sam? Did you like it as much as I did?" Ryan asked, his voice hoarse as he pulled me closer.

"I have nothing to compare it to. But I learned I enjoy being a power bottom as much as I enjoy being on top. I also liked you telling me what you wanted and me trying to oblige as much as I enjoy giving orders. That makes me feel well-rounded." I laughed. "I understand it's unusual for a guy to shoot his load just from being fucked, but that felt incredible. The bummer is we must be out of here in a few hours. I don't get to force-feed my load to you. There's little time left. I need to shower and pack. I don't want to wear my spunk dried up on my belly all the way home, and for you, probably another couple of days longer," I said as we unlocked ourselves from each other and got out of bed.

I stopped as a thought came to me. I didn't know why it hadn't occurred to me before now. I didn't know how Ryan would feel about it, but it seemed like a good idea given that it felt like neither Ryan nor I wanted to leave each other just yet.

I looked at him. "You know, Ryan, my Porsche made weird noises yesterday. It was popping like the fuel-air mixture wasn't quite right. It's still under warranty, so I think I should take it in because there won't be another city that can work on a Porsche between here and Lexington."

"Lexington?" he asked, surprise written all over his face.

"Yeah, I didn't want to give my final destination thinking you might be an ax murderer or stalker," I said, and he guffawed. "I know you're hurrying to get to your family, so I think I better stay, and you go on. I had the kitchen pack your lunch, which should help some," I told Ryan as I picked up the brown bag with his lunch.

"I thought that was one of the most beautiful-sounding engines I've ever heard, but y'all would know if it was sounding off. Well, I was looking forward to your company for the next several hours." Ryan looked genuinely disappointed. He had a very young, boyish-looking face that could show his thinking.

"Of course, if you don't mind the delay, you could wait with me and leave here in the morning. You could help find the Porsche dealership." Finally, I saw the light in his green orbs and the smile catching up.

"I reckon I could do that. When we return from the dealership place, we could watch a little television, and you could order dinner up here again tonight," he intoned as if testing the waters.

"Or, forget about the dealership, I'll call my dad telling him I'm staying here because of the work they need to do, and then go to a store and buy some beer and a box of extra-large condoms in case you decide to add to your sin list," I told him with a grin and a cheeky swagger to the shower.

"Well, reckon I can live with that. Under one condition," he added. "No more deals and no more ass whippings unless it's your ass that's getting whipped," he said and slapped my butt. I whooped and hopped into the shower.

"Agreed. No more deals and no ass whippings. We'll be two guys learning what the other likes," I agreed. My ass was still sore, and my dick a little tender, but I couldn't wait to get to that drugstore and load up on rubbers that fit both of us and some good quality lube. So we showered, laughing, with shampoo and soap bubbles everywhere. We were squeaky clean when we booked the room for Saturday night and again a late checkout Sunday afternoon. We stocked up on beer and whiskey and found an adult store where I bought some toys to play with and outfitted Ryan with a leather cock ring and a large bottle of the best lube they had. Looking like we cleaned the shelves at the sex toy store, we returned to the hotel with bags full of fun. We passed Evan, the bellhop, in the lobby. I smiled and spoke to the good-looking boy, who said to call him if he could do anything for us. Ryan asked who he was in the elevator, and I told him about Evan's earlier offer to be a third if we wanted him.

"The two of us can take care of everything we'd need him for," he said as he leaned over and kissed me until the elevator doors opened to our floor.

The next twenty-four hours convinced me I was

gay and liked it. We left just as the sun set the following day. Two hours later, we were in Lexington. Both had sore dicks, and our assholes were polished raw. The weekend's finality dragged us to the point of saying nothing, and when I suggested stopping by my old penthouse apartment so I could show him something, he readily agreed.

"Sit and wait here," I said as I pushed him down into the red leather couch in the corner of my spacious bedroom. I disappeared into my walk-in closet and selected some things. Then I went into my bathroom, changed clothes and did my hair. I combed my dark hair up into a widow's peak and wavy at the side, then twisted my bangs into a 1920s French Moulin Rouge style. A few minutes later I surprised Ryan by wearing my black satin lingerie. I trusted him and was eager to show him the last hidden truth about me.

His mouth opened and closed. His eyes stretched wider, but he seemed to compose himself after a few breaths as he eye-fucked me wearing my sexy hosiery, stockings, and heels. Hooded eyes and wordless affirmation of his acceptance made my heart flutter. After seeing him drool over my feminine accessorized body--my new black satin suspender belts, garters, and floral design panty-hose, I felt elated and confident.

Vulnerable, I knelt before him. His expression was predatorial hunger, just shy of snarling. Shakely, as if keeping himself from grabbing, he burrowed his fingernails into his upper legs. I reached over, unzipped his jeans, pulled his rosy pink well-used erection out, and gently started suckling the head, wetting, and blowing cool air over the tender flesh. When he came, the load was understandably smaller. So when he pulled me upward so I could straddle his legs, we had only a small taste of his essence to share, but he kissed me long and with a passion I'd never known before. We lay like that for about an hour, discussing what we learned from this weekend's experience. He confessed I had opened his eyes to a lot of kinks he had and felt he was a wiser man for it.

I surprised him by buying him a plane ticket from Lexington to Louisiana. He protested, saying it wasn't necessary and costing me too much. I told him he could repay me if he got back on his feet, but there was no obligation. Ryan said he would, and I gave him a cellphone number where he could reach me. I was too tired to drive, so I got him a taxi to the airport.

It was late Sunday night when I stood by the cab door. We gave each other a brief, manly hug.

"Good luck being a father. I hope you find what you're looking for," he said, his hand resting on my shoulder.

"I'm so glad I pulled over for you," I said, looking into those stunning eyes.

He smiled, cocking his head to the side as if reading me while beautiful blond hair cascaded over his angelic face. "You gave me so much more than I was looking for. Some truths to help me go on," he said with a smirk and got in the back seat of the taxi.

I watched it disappear down the lane.

Then it clicked—that cocky smirk.

It was the same all-knowing smirk he gave me when he'd gotten into my car.

Had he played with me? Was he the one who took me for a ride? I wondered for the next ten years while trying to forget him.

THE END...

To be continued in *Vampires Don't Drink Whiskey*.

About the Author

"I found it surprisingly beautiful. In a brutal, horribly uncomfortable sort of way." —Tyrion Lannister to Janos Slynt.

I am a Canadian speculative Male/Male Sci-Fi Fantasy and Paranormal Romance writer. I currently reside in the Rocky Mountains of beautiful British Columbia, Canada.

My writing explores who we are, where we come from, and where we are going as a human race on Earth.

I like to weave and bubblegum questions and subjects by creating new, exciting worlds and characters. My stories are unpredictable, twisted with a dash of humor, and centered on gay characters.

You will question your existence among these worlds and wish you could escape to these places filled with foul-mouthed heroes who struggle and strive to save humankind.

I hope you've discovered something that excites and intrigues you. Please share your thoughts by leaving a review or visit www.kashelchar.com to contact me or learn about my latest works.

www.ingramcontent.com/pod-product-compliance
Lightning Source LLC
Chambersburg PA
CBHW030536180626
46810CB00005B/1895